CAROL STREAM PUBLIC LIBRARY

3 1319 00500 3600

WITHDRAWN

W9-AMA-591

Very Hairy Bear

Alice Schertle

Illustrated by Matt Phelan

sandpiper

Houghton Mifflin Harcourt
Boston   New York

Carol Stream Public Library
Carol Stream, Illinois 60188-1634

Text copyright © 2007 by Alice Schertle
Illustrations copyright © 2007 by Matt Phelan

All rights reserved. Published in the United States by Sandpiper,
an imprint of Houghton Mifflin Harcourt Publishing Company.
Originally published in hardcover in the United States by Harcourt Children's Books,
an imprint of Houghton Mifflin Harcourt Publishing Company, 2007.

SANDPIPER and the SANDPIPER logo are trademarks of Houghton Mifflin Harcourt Publishing Company.

For information about permission to reproduce selections from this book, write to Permissions,
Houghton Mifflin Harcourt Publishing Company, 215 Park Avenue South, New York, New York 10003.

www.hmhbooks.com

The illustrations in this book were done in pastel and pencil on Rives BFK paper.
The display type was set in P22 Peanut.
The text type was set in Cheddar Salad.

The Library of Congress has cataloged the hardcover edition as follows:
Schertle, Alice.
Very hairy bear/Alice Shertle; illustrated by Matt Phelan.
p. cm.
Summary: Recounts the experiences of a shaggy, "boulder-big" bear as the four seasons
come to the beautiful wood which is his home.
[1. Bears—Fiction. 2. Seasons—Fiction.] I. Phelan, Matt, ill. II. Title.
PZ7.S3442Ve   2007
[E]—dc21 2003005888

ISBN: 978-0-15-216568-0 hardcover
ISBN: 978-0-547-72214-6 paperback

Manufactured in China
LEO 10 9 8 7 6 5 4 3 2 1

4500368183

E
Schertle, A

To Jen and Drew
John and Kate
Spence and Dylan
—A.S.

For Rebecca
—M.P.

12/12

Deep in the green gorgeous wood
lives a boulder-big bear
with shaggy, raggy, brownbear hair
everywhere...

except on his
no-hair
nose.

Each spring,
when the silver salmon leap into the air,
fisherbear is there

to catch them.

He stands in the river
with his brown coat dripping.

A very hairy bear
doesn't care
that he's wet.

Kerplunk!

He'll even dunk
his no-hair nose.

In it goes
when he smells *fish!*

Each summer,
he's a sticky, licky honey hunter,
with his bare nose deep
in the hollow of
a bee tree.

A very hairy bear
doesn't care
about stings and things.

Even on his no-hair nose.

When the summer blueberries
grow round and fat on their bushes,
a very hairy bear
doesn't care
that his nose gets blue.

He eats the berries and the bushes, too.
He's a very full

berryfull bear.

In the fall,

when quick gray squirrels hide acorns

under the oak trees,

a no-hair nose knows

where to find them.

A very hairy bear
doesn't care
if the squirrels scold.

He eats all the acorns
he can hold.

Then,

when soft white snowflakes start to fall
and cling to bear hair...

(if there's a bear there),

when fish sink to sleep deep in the pond,
wrapped in their silver scales,

and swarms of bees sleep
deep in their warm honey hives,

and squirrels lay curled
on heaps of nuts
in hollow trees,

he scratches his big brown bear behind
on the roughest tree trunk he can find,

and old big as a boulder bear
crawls deep into his cave.
He settles his big bear body down,
all covered up
by his bearskin coat,

all wrapped up
in his big hairy bearskin coat,

except

for his no-hair nose.

A very hairy bear
DOES care
about ice cold air
on his no-hair nose,

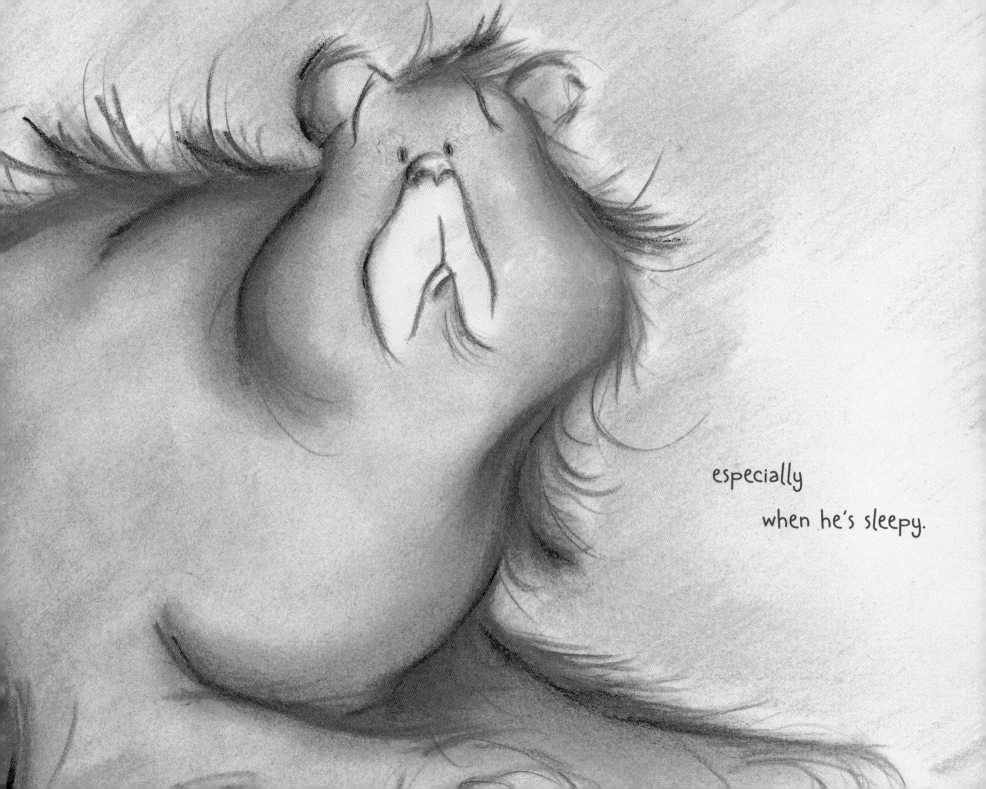

especially

when he's sleepy.

So,
he puts his big warm
bearpaws,

his shaggy, raggy,
very hairy
bearpaws
on top of his nose,

and goes

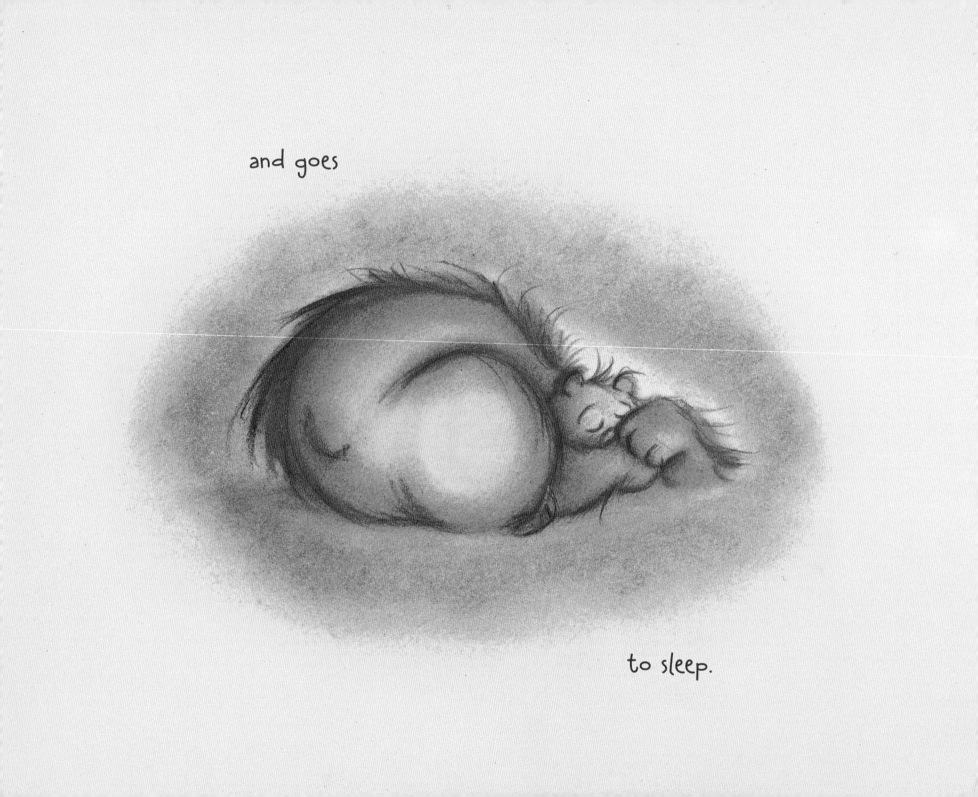

to sleep.